THE CRY WITHIN

By Stephen Elvis Otieno

A catalogue record for this book is available from the Kenya National Library Services.

ISBN 978-9966-020-71-0

E mail: stevelvis@gmail.com.

Cover illustration: Elis Otieno
Cover layout: Anthony waigwa
Cover design: Fred Sewe

This book is a work of fiction, any resemblance to actual persons living or dead is purely coincidental.

Acknowledgments

Glory is to God for the wisdom and inspiration of writing this book. I thank you my reader for choosing to journey with me through this book. My immense gratitude goes to my parents Thomas and Irene for showing me the way to school. Thank you to Mrs. Kariuki my high school teacher at Wareng high school – for believing in my writing skills. Many thank you to Mr. Peter Baumgartner who planted the germ of writing this book. Thank you to Laura Hodel, Alice Ndungu, Alicia Osiro and Clara Igobwa (Mrs.) for reading the manuscript and offering the necessary advice. And to my editors; Godiva Asiala Maloba, Mrs. Jennifer Thuo and James Kariuki of Mvule publishers it has always been a pleasure having you people. Thank you to my siblings Dennis, Beatrice, Mirriam, and Samuel for believing in me.

This novel could not have been published without the generous support of the parents of Logos Christian School, Nairobi, my counselors Jacinta Maiyo, Mr. Peter Kariuki and the Wahomes. Thank you to Mr. Machage Kisyeri, The Director-Genius Kings Schools –Tanzania, Mr. R.K Muzo, The director ADWEST LTD and Dennis Ochieng Otieno my dear brother for their generous support in the final production of this book. And finally, thank you to Grace Peter Kitila for bringing music to my life and being always beside me. I acknowledge countless individuals who shared their knowledge and expertise in the process of writing and final production of this book.

To Alvis; thank you for blessing my heart with the gift of faith.

To the children of the world from whom all grown-ups grew and to the grown- ups who were once children.

To the children of the world who perish in wars they no not about, in loving memory.

Stephen Elvis Otieno was born in 1983. He studied at Wareng High school Eldoret, Egoji teachers college and Kenya Institute of Professional counseling/Kenya Methodist University, where he studied medical health and psychology. He is currently a student at Africa Nazarene University.

Stephen is a member of the Depth Alliance of Psychology and Inter Religious Council for Peace. He has written poems, plays and Narratives and is featured in the Parents Magazine May 2008 issue as a survivor in the post election violence in Kenya. Stephen is a crusader for human rights and has worked with United States Peace Corps as a life skills trainer, Avalain computer –Germany and Switzerland. He has participated in Social Psychology training in the faculty of social psychology in the Wesleyan University and the faculty of clinical psychology in the University of Edinburgh. Stephen has taught and has been a leader and life skills trainer in different institutions in East Africa.

THE CRY WITHIN

By Stephen Elvis Otieno

1

THERE I WAS, right in the middle of a freezing morning cold which threatened to take away my life. I was shivering and it was easy to notice how the coldness was eating my flesh. I looked confused and torn between two worlds; a world of reality and a world of fantasy. *Did I hear him?* Yes! I must have heard my son's request, his words cut across my tiny womb like a double edged sword. It was like I was in the middle of a dream or some sort of a nightmare. I felt like I was the main character in a book full of dramatic scenes and painful moments, a book where most of the characters are not quite sure of life.

I would prefer reading charming and entertaining books, books about adventures and animals. Unfortunately the characters in the book are like me, lifeless characters who go through torture and pain at a tender age. I would prefer not to speak, for I can't speak now. *Would I recommend you reading such a book?* I can't make any suggestions. Reading such a book would make you feel the heat in the cold just like I felt in the freezing morning at the camp. I was in the middle of somewhere, not quite sure where I was. It could have been at the edge or the middle of the camp. *Did I have a choice?* I thought. *No!* I had no choice but to be at the camp.

I stood at the edge of a footpath that seemed heading to nowhere. Some stench hung in the air. The stench was awful but I had to cope up with it for as long as I was at the camp. What was visibly in front of me was a symbol of "hope". It was not comparable to what I had seen at home, where children were bulleted and beheaded in full glare of their mothers, expectant mothers having their wombs disemboweled, young girls and women ravished in light. The stack of bodies laying down staring back with dullness as if asking why lack of peace had robbed them their lives was still fresh in my memories.

There I was, as if drowning in the morning cold. My legs felt weak moving awkwardly like a marionette, I felt disconnected from my body. It was like I was swimming to uncertainty, trying to rescue myself from the raging water that threatened to wash away my body. I felt like the last survivor in the sinking titanic.

In the freezing morning the camp was waking up; but that does not mean that she had slept all night. My eyes took a snap shot of what was visibly around me, they did not play me false; I saw what I was meant to see. The refugee camp was full of life and the business of everyday was beginning to take shape and form.

I watched dead bodies stack up like firewood ready for mass burial. I watched children on their mothers back crying for food, denied the joy of childhood and being eaten up by starvation; not with a trace of any going to school. I could hear the usual screams here and there; see men and women dancing the tunes of *Muratina* a local brew, maybe trying to forget the circumstances which were eating their soul of souls. As usual I saw men seated on stones discussing the politics of the day and admiring young girls and women.

The camp was unusually cold and freezing, in most cases it had always been hot and dusty. Poverty had squarely and romantically embraced the camp and mostly we depended on the food ration by WFP.

Hungry men, protruding ribs of children and bare chest of women revealed the magnitude of starvation that was threatening to swallow up the whole camp. Up and down walked the army's special envoys deployed to keep vigil and protect us from the snares and gunfire that had become the order of the day. *They were peace keepers, but was there peace to keep?* The life in the camp was a replica of how hell must look.

I stood still gazing at the day's dramas which were unfolding in front of me. I reached into my pocket and removed the creased laboratory test report. Running my eyes through it, there was no doubt it was hard to understand what was clearly visible in front of my tiny eyes- I was not expecting it of course! My eyes staggered through the report whose language I could not understand. The black writings on the white sheet of paper made me crazy. I struggled not to cry but my tear glands finally gave up the ghost and burst their banks sending jets of tears down my cheeks at a frightening rate.

Then came the dark memory of the usual gunfire at Changaraweni which was deafening, the screams and the wailing of children and women were equally deafening. Like a strike of a match stick it all began with indifference in political opinion, then it boiled hot to quarrels and fights and graduated to gunfire, brutal killings and murder. By the end of it all, devastating deaths and trauma of the highest magnitude, dead bodies lain down unsure of their fate, families displaced and properties destroyed, and young children orphaned at their earliest age. At Changareweni everything had been reduced to rubles, young men and women supporting either side of a political divide crisscrossed the city and destroyed virtually everything in their wake.

The refugee camp had been set for those who would be alive; it was a resting place for the dead and the dying. My first steps to the camp were like that of a child unsure of her footings. Our Journey was like an old time exodus to the *Promised Land.* The mass movement was a true proof of people running to safeguard their lives.

On our way we stepped on bodies, dead bodies staring at us full of hope; not one, not two but countless bodies. Death had often gazed at us and parted friends and neighbors from each other. Home literary smelled death, we left fresh graves that spoke the statement; if you liked hell you will like Changaraweni.

There I was, weakened by my situation, making one step at a time towards school. My feeble legs could not take it anymore and as they fought with my weight, I landed on a rock near a pool of water. For nearly a fortnight, I had grappled and fought with my thoughts over my state and I was now holding the reality in my watery hands drenched with sweat in the morning cold. Looking at the report again, I hated it and wondered why the doctor did not use a computer in this age and time; perhaps it would look presentable if he had typed the report. I wondered why in the digital age some parts of this sub-Saharan world were still dancing the analogue tunes.

The result of the laboratory test was far from real. It was an awful experience that had gone worse. I stared in horror at the piece of paper documenting my state of pregnancy. My name was correctly tagged on it... Zawadi Simba. My age was rightly written; 13 years old. Some crooked writings followed. Then the real shock hit my head like a gunshot few meters away. Pregnancy test result: Positive! *This is madness! Or is it some sort of idiocy?* I deliberated and shoved it in the torn pocket of my school uniform as I continued sitting on the rock. "You are pregnant" The doctor's words hit my mind again. This time the reality was real. *Good Lord!* I dropped, *what is this anyway?*

Three fine days had elapsed without a drop of proper food into my belly; my stomach was dry, I was not only hungry but literary starving! My body was resting down on the rock, a worried girl wondering why the world had turned its ugly face on me. Looking at a still pool of water in front of me, it was calm; there was no noise from it. The peace it enjoyed was disturbing and I took it that the living creatures in it were peaceful too.

Why would such creatures enjoy their freedom while I grapple with lots of pain? I thought. A butterfly settled peacefully on a beautiful red rose beside me. *I will kill it.* I contemplated. I slowly crept and caught it, looked up and talked to the wise one. *Thank you heavens for bringing such a beautiful creature into being,* I said carefully holding it in my hands. *You are surely a gift,* I said.

With a passionate admiration I let it fly. The birdlike creature winged its winglets round my head time and again. It flapped its red "wings" which had white spots. It was a real beauty! Spreading its fragrance and enjoying its short life on the cruel earth. It then settled on my palm. *Oh, crap!* I killed it with cruelty of my thoughts at that moment, dismembering the head the thorax and the abdomen, pulling out the winglets with a lot of cruel passion.

Lamentations of killing such a beautiful small "bird" crisscrossed my mind. *Is it a sin?* My mind sought to confirm. I was not sure of whether I committed a sin or a crime. *Is it a crime?* No! The little creature did not deserve any life while I was lifeless.

My decrepit legs knelt down; I picked a stone and hit the pool to disrupt the peace it was enjoying. Everything had to be like me for the life in me was worth no life. *Why would they burn our houses? Why would they destroy the peace we had enjoyed for long? Why would they render my friends speechless, kill and ravish their mothers and daughters? Why would they maim their fathers and steal their properties? Why...? Why...?* I thought. I kept on playing memories after memories and wondered why I was holed in that hell of a camp called Busutamu.

2

BUSUTAMU CAMP translated as sweet kiss stood majestically at the western end of the country's capital. The non-classical architectural structures were accurately designed to echo the living standards of the people of Busutamu. Lain on an expansive plain, the extent of the dilapidated tents and muddy structures could be seen from a distant. The makeshift tents painted the whole of Busutamu camp white while the muddy structures painted her brown. She was a city within a city; a haven to some and a place where many people called home.

Busutamu had emerged to be one of the largest shanty residences in the country. Whenever I thought about her, sickness and diseases painted my thoughts. It was easy to notice children dropping dead from cholera and diarrhea, men and women overwhelmed by TB trying hard to breathe, young energetic men and girls dropping down with Ebola and scores of people nursing bullet wounds and *panga,* machete cuts.

Against a backdrop of misfortunes, poverty and fear of death; people's hearts were full of vision, resilience and hope that someday under the sun, the gods of the daughters and the sons of the soil would hear their story. They were hopeful that someday dusk would dawn and their cry world would end.

The camp was on a plain; whenever you were up a hill side you could see her spread her taste of beauty. This was a small island of paucity found in the blackened seas of infinity. There is where I had called home in the aftermath of war at Changaraweni.

Still seated on the rock, my thoughts were rendered caged as I remembered the tragic demise of my mother who passed on without telling me the secret of the family curse, which lain within her heart; the secret behind my identity which I was seeking to find. My mother a staunch believer of her private life, could not let me play or even walk with children of my neighborhood. At my early years I could hang around with Maimuna a young girl who was equally my age-We were all five years old. My mother moved to changareweni when I was two years old. Though Changarewni had united people of all walks of life, the people were divided along tribal lines, race, colour and religion. My mother constantly reprimanded me against playing with Maimuna because she did not belong to my religion.

Most of the time; I unconsciously ignored my mother's reprimands and found myself playing with Maimuna and our other friends. Most of the time we made small dolls and small planes made of paper. We flew the planes, nursed our babies and watched our elder friends playing *dame* and *kati* some simple games. We made balls using old socks and young boys made theirs using plastic bags.

Karish one of the young boys in his mid-childhood always led us to the nearest river for a "swimming" gala locally known as *duduf mpararo.* We could play over and over again oblivion of any difference until it was time to go home. I always remember when the older friends would go up a hill and slide down using old plastic cans. They took turns as we watched and cheered. I continued playing knowing well that what awaited me at home meant death. That was it- a typical childhood. Then it happened;

"I want you to listen to this," My mother said after giving me a thorough beating.

"I don't want you to play with them again, they are not of your religion and tribe and they will teach you bad manners." She continued.

My mother then imposed a curfew on me and before long we shifted deeper into Changaraweni. For long, I felt lonely since I could not play with Maimuna and my friends again.

I had been taught that in the beginning of time people lived together in harmony and peace. The atmosphere was full of love. They traded together and cultivated together. People owned cattle and sheep and gave God sacrifices to bless their land. That was not real in my life, for time had changed and the fabric of unity within people had been eaten up by giants called tribalism, war and racism. What had been left was mere shadow of people's former selves. Sometimes life is like watching a never ending movie full of dramatic scenes in which we are the main characters. The love and peace that was within the hearts of people has been replaced by animosity and blackened hearts. *Now this part of sub-Saharan world was at war with herself.* I thought.

There I was, wondering why my mother allowed me to face the full havoc of life. There I was, drenched with sweat in the freezing morning. The images of babies being thrown into pit latrines, families being broken, children being subjected to war, corporal work and terror, and people being judged not by the content of their character but by the colour of their skin, by the language and tribe of their tongue and by their status of life constantly nagged my brain.

There I was, representing the children of Africa and the world who are continuously subjected into torture, war and death, children- pregnant with hope but confronted with war and terror. On the rock I sat representing the children with a bright future, going through all sorts of problems staring out at the world with glaring eyes for help. There I was representing children who were fatherless.

Though I had never set my eyes on my father, my mother had always talked about him. I remembered his name *"Ben!"* Yes Ben- that was his name. You see, it is like I was crazy! My brain had been eaten up by my situation and circumstances. I wished my father was there to stand by my side in the circumstance that was silently eating up my soul of souls. I wished that the fore fathers of our nations who fought the good fight would rise up and confront the tyrannies that threatened to eat up the children of the world. I wished that the fore mothers of our nations and all the mothers of peace were there to embrace me and give me a chance to live my life.

There I was an IDP; a refugee in my own mother land wondering when I would start living and stop drowning in the flood of rhetoric promises.

My stomach was still wobbling and grumbling wishing I could get something in my mouth that early morning. If wishes were horses then beggars would ride. Had I got raw meat, it would have been as sweet as honey. My hands would grab it and my teeth tear it into small pieces. My teeth ground with anger as I tried my best to keep warm inside my torn school uniform. My body was inside a patched pair of full dress, a pair of socks that had not known water for some days, black shoes that had turned brown and a big school bag on my back. My swollen eyes continued to give way to tears dropping down my cheeks escorted by the drizzles that embraced my face passionately.

I threw my head down as if in a world of my own. It was as if I was mad, yes, maddened by the deafening inner noise that had engulfed my brain. I remembered my state of pregnancy, this time the reality was hitting me hard second by second! *How am I going to deal with it? How am I going to deal with this horrific creature inside me? How do I deal with the horrific images that are eating the better part of my being? Isn't this a nightmare?* I thought. No one was ready to listen to my story. It was as if I was ending my story, but that is just how I was beginning it. It was against myriads of thoughts that I made steps towards school.

3

MAPOROMOKO SCHOOL in the heart of Busutamu was going to be my destination; a ten kilometer walk that my frail feet knew too well. The rough terrains of Busutamu had known my legs for some time. I had developed a special relationship with the dilapidated paths that strongly missed me on the days I missed school. Sometimes I could take the long path on the *untarmacked* tarmac and watch vehicles sway their ways into the camp. Sometimes I could take the ever winding foot paths, jump the blackened riverine whose water was flowing from upstream and content myself with the stench that came from the open sewers downstream. Mostly I managed without a stumble or two on the way, but sometimes I was unlucky.

Being the brightest girl in my class, the green leaf was slowly changing its colour. I watched my dream of being a lawyer and a human rights activist fade away like a distant mirage. I would dream of protecting the rights of children and take to book all the defilers of girls and boys. My dreams were being shattered under my watch and my heart was in the verge of breaking like a piece of glass dropped from a cliff and falling on the rough terrain of the earth's surface.

It was true my life was a nightmare, an everlasting nightmare! *How will I cope with my class mates laughing at me? What would be going through my class teachers mind when she gets to know?* The gnawing feeling kept coming back to me taking the better part of my thoughts. I was always a mirror; nearly all my class mates viewed their academic life through me. There I was, viewing myself through the broken pieces of my own mirror of life.

While I made smaller strides and sometimes bigger strides, a shrill of jitters ran through my blood as my memory deliberated on the teacher on duty; Mr. Bokasa. Being of tough character, energetic and corpulent, he earned a nickname, *Kisu*, a knife. He accepted the nickname, not that he liked it with a passion, but he knew that it came from his trepidating character. His blood was forcefully flowing in my tiny womb a month and some days since it happened.

I bore the secret that only my heart and the little creature growing in my womb knew. Drizzles started beating the earth; I then sought refuge in an amorphous shelter along the way. I decided to sit on a bench right in the middle of the shelter. The memories of how it happened flashed back.

"*Goond* morning *crass*, *totay* we are *tiscussing sakos*," Mr. Kisu greeted us with a high pitched voice that broke the silence we were enjoying and with a funny accent that painfully tortured my ears.

"A *sako* is something *sakula*, but first let us *traw* …," he continued to teach the math lesson. I then raised my hand. "Escuse me *mwalim* I have not caught there," I asked. "Where…?" He asked.

"There...," I said pointing at the blackboard.

"Zawadi *sikuelewi*, I don't understand you, *mbona unaletako fitu fichinga fichinga?* Why are you behaving like a fool?" He said.

The whole class roared into laughter.

"*Mnacheka*! Are you laughing at me? I will work on your backs!" He continued.

Mr. Kisu was one man known for taking his jokes seriously and that day he was not going to disappoint. He took a whip and gave everybody three strokes of cane on their backs, fortunately I was lucky.

In my cogitation, the rains beat periodically forming a nice rhythm. The torrential rain was falling hitting the earth with its entire wrath. Mr. Kisu was teaching me mathematics in his office. It was a remedial lesson on fractions and algebra. The tuition took too long. Then whatever transformed resurfaced in my memory and I felt like it was happening again. I should have known something was wrong when I entered his office, I should have looked at the closed windows and known that trouble was eminent. I was like a lamb taking herself to the slaughter house!

"*Mara mocha tu zawadi unachua unakuanga msupuu Sana*-Just once Zawadi, you know you are very beautiful," he said drawing closer to me.

"What?" I exclaimed.

"I wonder if anyone has ever told you that you must be the most beautiful woman on earth," he said trying to put his hands over my shoulders.

"Teacher, please no!" I exclaimed.

"Nobody will know, Zawadi you are so sweet." he said trying to grab me.

"What is the meaning of this?" I asked.

I struggled with him but he overpowered me. He grabbed my hand and held me tight trying to lay my body on his office desk. With a lot of energy my body brought itself up against the goliath of a man, it was as though some deep artesian well had been struck in my soul of souls and strength came forth. When I stood up, my tiny body was now face to face with him. He looked out through the window and then back at me. I could neither wail nor scream. Looking at the door, there was no room to escape. A shudder of fear rocked my body. Then followed some sounds of turning tables. My assailant did not stop, instead he grabbed my tiny body again and this time my energy gave in to his energy. My cry was overshadowed by the fury of rain that was beating the earth. "*Ukicharipu kusema nitakuua* ; if you dare to report I shall kill you," he roared.

The thunderous voice beat my ears, his words scaring as I lay down on the floor. It was as if I was swimming in my own pool of blood. So powerless and overwhelmed I was that I could not cry any more. My assailant ran to the door and wiped the blood in a hurry. He wiped his sweat and held me by his arm like a hungry hunter who had caught a prey.

The drizzle subsided and I opened my eyes. It was like watching one of those slow-motion scenes in a movie, the kind of you know what is going to happen next, but are powerless to prevent it. I felt dejected and no one could define what was gnawing my soul. It was like being an actor in an African horror play. I felt angry about everything, angry that I was a statistic of victims of rape.

Still seated on the bench, I inserted my hands in my school bag and removed a sheet of paper which had a poem that I had presented in the interschool poetry competition. I emerged the best poet but my school did not have enough money to finance my progress to the next level. My eyes staggered through the words of the poem as I read:

"I speak about the dispeakable
Actions that are intolerable
Occurrence that is horrible
Pressure that is unbearable
But no one seems answerable so I speak

I speak about the truth hidden
Monsters roam the garden of humanity
Young apples unripe bitten
With bites of cruelty
The attack is always sudden
With moves of insanity
So I speak

I speak against vultures that sneak
Beneath children's pillows
Traumatizing their dreams
Into nightmares
Their playgrounds to fields of disaster
Their vision to confusion

From tender veins blood is oozing

Their cries all agonizing

The silence is bitter amazing

I speak against silence that laden!

Will you speak if it strikes?

Will you speak for me?

For us?

Will you speak?"

The words of the poem were so real in my life. This time there was no one to clap for me for a splendid performance on the stage, instead my eyes gave way to tears that run down my chicks like a river that had burst her banks.

I touched my belly and thought of removing the growing thing in my womb for that was the order of the day at the refugee camp. *I am in this situation because of my state of pregnancy! How am I different from the girls who have been throwing their fetus in the latrines? How am I different from the girls who have been throwing their fetus in the bush, in the rivers, leaving them to rot in the forest?* I thought. But it is not allowed unless a written law permits it. It is a crime they say.

While my heart was willing to go to school, my legs refused. I wondered what would happen at the end of the year when the form one entry exams called. I wondered how I would journey myself through my state of pregnancy in the kind of life I was going through- the kind, where the next meal was a mirage, the kind, where life in itself was threatening. *This is a kind of slavery* I thought.

Should I manage to stay at school, how will I contain Mr. Kisu? The mentioning of his name pierced my heart and it was now soaked with blood. I was tired of school; I was tired of seeing other girls my age being ideal candidates of a situation I was going through, a situation and a circumstance that had now become part of me. I fought with the thought of not going to school but finally my legs agreed after a long deliberation. I was now willing to face that man I called teacher. Meanwhile thoughts ran over in my mind.

Suppose I journey through my pregnancy and give birth to a baby boy? Though I would love to hate my assailant with a passion, I had a liking for a boy child even as I believed that the faint tremors of the life nudging the inside of my soft belly would finally see the light of the day. I believed I would bring forth a man who will stand firm as a well anchored corner post and fight for his sisters and mothers. I believed I would bring forth a man who would be a benchmark in life, society and family.

I believed I would bring forth a man who would exercise his masculine responsibility, demonstrate strength and stability to protect and provide for those within his sphere of influence. But how would I provide for him and fulfill my desire? At my age I had nobody by my side. Those called to protect me had turned against me *No! I must remove him whether the law permits or not. I will have broken the law but not committed a crime, I must remove him,* I thought.

I had believed that my name was misplaced and if there was any power in names, then not mine. Being called *Taabu*, which means trouble, would be my preference. Well I thought Taabu or trouble should have been my middle name. My life was much more of "*Taabu*" than "*Zawadi.*"

Step by step I moved towards school. The luggage behind me was very heavy, a huge bag, inside it crumpled books with missing pages. No text books but a dish and a plate. Thank God for the food for all; an education initiative by World Food Programme.

As I approached the school, my legs became heavy and I could not walk. The little creature in my womb refused, it jumped. As if I was dreaming, I imagined my son going to Maporomoko school, late for school and Mr. Kisu was on duty. Undoubtedly there would be eminent danger. Mr. Kisu would be literally at the gate waiting for the late comers, behind him a long whip of "*nyahunyo*," a snake like whip made of rubber from a car tyre. He would be in his popular suit that he had inherited from his late brother.

"Bahati," the rough voice of Mr. Kisu would roar, "You are late again!" He would utter making advancement towards him. His veins already out and the black eyes open behind the dark membranes giving way to expanding pupils. It would be certain that he would have launched an attack of the times on my son and the cannons of justice fully loaded. His tongue would flicker and sway in and out emitting the fang of words. My son would be quiet, watching the teacher making his advancement wishing that the grace of God could fall on him.

"You think I am your father, do I look like him?" the thunderous voice would beat his ears like thunderstorm on a stormy day. "No Sir," He would reply meekly with hands behind his back.

Back to my senses, I could not imagine how fast I arrived at the school. As if it was true, I found Mr. Kisu at the gate with a *nyahunyo*, sixteen pupils were kneeling on the earthen floor. He let me in and allowed me to go to class never uttering a word. I looked at him with all the hatred aware that his blood was forcefully flowing in my womb. I believed he was not only crazy but evil. I believed that one day the full arm of law will catch on him. As I headed to the classroom, I looked back and he looked back at me with a dull stare. *When I will get to know my father, I will tell him all that happened to me.* I thought. Anger piled up inside me, I hated the stare, I spat so that the wind could taste my fury.

4

THE SIGHT OF MR. KISU made me hate school, but undoubtedly, it was the passion for knowledge that had pulled my legs to school. I stood, taking a deep breath with my heart counting the beats one at a time; I made one stride after another towards school. It was like walking on the surface of the moon where one is scared of being pulled up to infinity. I knew that the next eight months and counting would be the most horrifying moments of my lifetime. My state of pregnancy and my state of life continued to render me hopeless.

The dull picture of the school surrounded me like total darkness in the wee hours of a cold night. The dilapidated gate that was dancing to the grounds, the mad walled classrooms roofed with rusted iron sheet that chocked when we were in, the blackboard that was trying to save itself from the raging termites and the earthen floor that housed the hungry jiggers proved the state of our school at its best. It was built on a small piece of land. Some of the classes had plywood and sacks as their walls. The local area MP Hon. Goto Gototo grabbed part of the land set aside for expansion. As the minister of lands, he used his influence in the government to take the land and built a multimillion office next to the school, for he wanted to be closer to the people.

The ever locked office was gathering dust and the padlock had now rusted. The only person who could be seen in the compound was *Mzee* Magwanda, a renowned old man in the village who was employed as a guard. The classes were overstretched beyond their capacity. Sometimes we could study under a fruitless mango tree we called *muembe gumba*. Everything looked substandard save for the staffroom which had two desks and a chair for the seven teachers. The window was wooden and covered with a plastic paper that served as glass.   There, teachers took tea and enjoyed the politics of the land. The staff room was nicknamed "parliament" by pupils simply because politics was at its best there.

I pulled my eyes and a dozen of queries rocked my mind as I saw the teachers in the staffroom. I then considered indulging my curiosity to the conversations. "How do you see that class seven girl?" Mr. Shimwero asked. It dawned on me that there was yet another prospective victim to follow my path. I frowned and then chose to disapprove the sentiments...

I could hear the conversation over and over as I passed by the staffroom heading to my class. Next to the staffroom were the head teacher's office and his deputy's that served also as the senior teacher's office.

Mr. Kisu was the senior teacher. Mr. Kisu and the head teacher had disagreed over their positions and constantly had supremacy battles with teachers taking either side.

The government had provided books to be issued to us as a free primary education initiative but this was only on paper. In practical our schools bookstore had mostly old syllabus books, which still looked very new.

Behind the classes there was a small playground meant for Physical Education lessons that were never taught. Teachers used the time to complete the syllabus that was never completed. The playground also served as the assembly ground where the scouts hoisted the torn flag every Monday and Friday and it also hosted major functions like closing days and fundraisers.

Mrs. Wambete our class teacher was in class. Our lovely Mum as we called her was old enough to be our grandmother. The grey hair on her head could reveal that. She was a teacher who we never had wanted to loose, for she treated us like her own grandsons and daughters. In her sunset days in the field of teaching, nothing bothered her. Her moods were elevated when word came around that the government had extended the retirement age for teachers from fifty-five to sixty years.

She was one happy woman for in six years she would still chalk and talk. She was never bothered by our endless noise and laughter and the jokes that we made about her. It was only one occasion when she was really upset that we knew the other side of her for the better. One boy had pinched the other for cutting a piece of his *mandazi,* an African bun. The thunder of laughter awakened the teacher from her slumber. In amazement and shock, the poor teacher stood appalled in front of us. The thunder of laughter continued. Suddenly her hands started shaking like a seal. She went out and lay in grass looking as if she was about to erupt into tears. We felt so remorseful. Our class prefect went and held her hands to support her. We promised her to be good forever.

Mrs. Wambete had already called the register before my arrival. She had marked me absent for she had not felt my presence in the class. The class was pregnant with laughter, no one could hold. Pupils laughed wildly rendering me hostage and confused.

"So you are here," She said wearing a plastic smile. She was a woman of few words.

"Nthen ngo and sit ndown", she ordered me to sit.

The desk that was meant to accommodate three was now forced to stretch to accommodate the six of us.

On the timetable, it was time for Science. Many pupils liked this subject so much. The topic of the day was reproduction in animals. "When a male and a female reproductive cell meet, reproduction takes place," Mrs. Wambete explained. The teacher continued talking about reproduction amidst laughter. It was as if the teacher was speaking the unspeakable words.

"What are the signs of pregnancy?" She asked.

"Yes Zawadi" She pointed at me.

I stood to answer but words could not come out of my mouth. I felt like an arrow was piercing my heart instead, I stood like a statue staring right at the teacher. It was a shame that a bright girl like me did not know the signs of pregnancy. Well she chose to ignore me and continued with the lesson. My wits drove me crazy and I could not take it anymore. *I must remove this creature that has denied me the freedom of enjoying my childhood.* I thought. I felt like hating and hitting everyone so hard but I did not have the energy.

Mrs. Wambete had given us class work. She was now sewing her basket that she sold every market day. I took my Social Studies book to read. I loved Social Studies for it taught me about the beautiful world, our land and culture, and about the rights of children. I opened the page on children's rights; "Right to education, protection and respect" I nodded my head in affirmation asking myself when I would begin to enjoy the rights.

The next page drove my thoughts crazy. I saw a photograph of two women standing and a man squatting between them. On the right was a lady I had never seen, but on the left was my mother a slimy young woman whose life was cut short by the crude hands of the assailants during the war.

My mum was a scholar and a graduate from Kisuma University where she studied Political Science and graduated with first class honors. In the photograph, she looked young and beautiful, without blemish or spot. Her deep dimples revealed her beauty and the earrings that were now stack on her ears told more about her. The white blouse in a black blazer and skirt complemented her. In her hand, she held a book entitled *Effects of political violence to children.*

Her feet were housed by high-heeled shoes that showed her smooth round legs. Next to her and very close was a man. He was in blue jeans trousers and a blue shirt. He was wearing a cap and black shoes. Though he looked familiar one would be forgiven to believe it was Mr. Kisu. On the right was a woman who was equally beautiful. She was rather dark in color. I looked behind the picture and the following words met my eyes written in bold, **"Purity when she was three months pregnant …looking is Ben Simba."** *could Ben be my real father?* I sought to confirm but there was nobody to answer my question. It was like being in a thick and dark forest lost in the woods. "Ben" I said looking at the photo, *I don't know whether to love you or hate you,* I thought. *But my mum's name is Gracie and not Purity.* I thought. I looked at the photo a second time and with that glance, a thousand memories came back.

I had gone home late after the sports. Sure of getting my mum at home, I pushed the wooden door and it swung itself wide open. It was dark in the house, save for the hungry flame of *kanyitira*, a tin lamp that stood still in the air. The darkness was feeling and nothing moved. In the quietness, I could hear some sounds. I felt relieved when I realized that my mother was in the room.

"Zawadi my daughter are you back from school?" She asked.

"Yes mum" I answered.

"Any porridge mum? I am very hungry." I enquired.

"No sugar and flour my child, but I shall go to work, I shall bring you *mandazi*," she uttered as her tear dropped.

My mother was an eloquent speaker. She was a linguist and was so fluent in English. A very learned woman she was but her prospects of getting a job were eroded away by the flood of poverty. She always encouraged me to work hard in school. That day there was no much talk with her. She was not feeling well. She served me dinner of mashed potatoes. I then opened my book to do my Social Studies homework. The *kanyitira* finally emitted its final flame. I then dozed off on the wooden couch that danced to the ground as if it was going to die the next minute.

Suddenly the usual happened. I heard some sounds from a far and then it came nearer and nearer. I lifted my head to focus my ears, *No! Not again!* The rain of gunshots pierced my heart; the frightening sounds of the ceaseless attacks surrounded me like a rough sheet of noise.

I heard shootings from a far and from the rooftops and on the streets "Slash...Slash...Slash..." then followed by a deep silence as if nothing had happened. They were at it again. I prayed that nothing would happen to us. In the secret hour, in the darkness of night I could hear, "*mshike, mshike*"catch him catch him. They were close to three hundred men holding *pangas* machetes and *rungus*, clubs. They then began to chant:

Tumewaua,tumewaua

haki yetu,haki yetu

haki yetu haki yetu.

We have killed them, we have killed them

Our right, our right

Our right, our right

My mother then woke up from her slumber and held me tight by her side. I looked at her and tears started dripping down my eyes. I was too young to comprehend what was happening. Women were wailing, children crying, dogs barking the barking of the dogs forming a wailing rhythm. *"Hao si kabila yetu* those are not of our tribe,'' they shouted.

The smell of gunshots reached our house at last. I took a deep breath, and then suddenly the big bang was real. The men were literary in front of us. I was about to watch a live movie packed with action. They grabbed my mum and when I looked behind it was a face that I had seen almost every day. Mikosi Our neighbour, the charcoal dealer was holding my mum's hand tightly. I thought he had come to our rescue, I was wrong. He gave me a heavy slap on my face that rendered me unconscious. When I regained consciousness, I was literary on the ground. My mum's mouth was full of soil, her ears had maize grains and so were the nostrils. I had no voice to cry, I stood ready to attack. I took the cooking stick and tried to hit Mr. Mikosi. Another man strangled me from behind and covered my mouth with a dirty handkerchief as they repeatedly ravished my mother in the full glare of my watch.

They then left as if they had done nothing. I was left helpless as I watched my lovely mum grappling with pain. She fought for her dear life but the pain was too much. She gulped her last air and off she went.

In her mind I knew she wanted us to go together to the land of no return. Her body was laid to rest in a mass grave provided by the state. But she left me to tell the story.

"Zawadi …Zawadi…Zawadi…" I could hear her call. The echo of her voice was so real as if she was alive. "Zawadi….Zawadi….Zawadi …!" It was Mrs. Wambete calling from behind, I was alone and everyone had already left the class. With tears rolling down my cheeks, my head shaking and my book wet, I took a pen turned the picture and wrote: "I love you Mum beyond my last breath." Looking at Mrs. Wambete's old eyes as they met my tender eyes, tears continued dripping like torrential rain and my internal noise more than that of *vuvuzela.* "Talk to me my daughter, I am all ears," She told me as she drew closer to me. For a moment, I began to feel that she was the shield that my body needed when I was fighting for my dear life in the hands of my assailant-Mr. Kisu. After a long silence and continual pursuance from her, I felt like giving in and telling her the story. But my trust was all gone.

I must remove this tiny creature and nobody should know, my thoughts confirmed.

"I am o.k." I said.

"You can always count on me," she said as she left. *"Can I? No! Today I must remove it whether the law permits or not, I must remove it.*

In the mean time a clique of my classmates had gathered around me. Within minutes, the entire school was around me. I lifted up my eyes and wondered why the crowd was around me. It was like I had called for a magic show. One of the girls; though I could not figure out who, read aloud my name and my state of pregnancy. The dull voice surrounded me like a red blanket of noise and it was followed by a loud noise from the pupils standing in front of me and from others behind me. I froze like a corpse.

Then the school bell rang ushering in the beginning of another class session and the madness of rushing towards the classes filled the air. I dipped my hand into my pocket and the paper that contained the pregnancy test results was missing.

Within a few minutes, I was alone again. Looking behind I could see the pupils peeping through the window looking at me.

I speak not, I work not
See fingers pointing by
While children leap and die;
I see armies of flies fly
Celebrating over our lips in limbo
And even in death they celebrate
Terrain of humanity like a jumbo lie in waste
Wasted child! Wasted child!
Oh, with this waste should I speak?

I thought of the words of the popular poem and maybe in a situation like that, that was when it was written. It was like I was thrown in a bottomless dungeon of problems.

I carried myself heading towards nowhere. My mornings of endless light, had turned to nights of endless darkness. *What will I tell my uncle and his cruel wife? (My uncle Pastor Muema is a noble man.) Why the shame?* In a moment, I found myself in the ladies washroom. Digging deep in my bag I found some drugs I had hidden in case I made up my mind to terminate the pregnancy. I looked up and saw a penknife that had stayed there for some days. "This is the best tool to terminate this pregnancy," I said lifting my heavy body to pick it. Suddenly I heard a faint voice, followed by thunderous cough. One would think that there was a person being strangled in the next room. Questions raged my mind and I did not know what to do. The coughing became persistent then suddenly subsided. *Has she gone out?*

I ran to the room where the coughing came from and kicked the door. There was no one, but a pool of blood which greeted my eyes. A short silence was followed by a loud cry of a baby. *Am I dreaming?* I stood aghast with the knife in my hand. I looked again but I could not see anybody. I got out and used the outer "gate" to the cask of wasteland I called home.

5

I HAD DECIDED NOT TO GO HOME STRAIGHT. On my way I found myself near a cemetery. It was full, a sign that the dead were becoming more than the living. I then sat down and unfathomable memory of my mum came to life and the bitterness of tribalism and political violence, war and terror beat with my heart but never wishing that the living being in my tiny womb would go through the pain and agony I was facing. I then knelt down, collected some soil and started my talk with God.

For a long time I remained silent and even tried to understand what that meant to me. But its complications made me feel like giving up everything I had if any including my life. At thirteen, I was already facing the better share of life with no one in the vicinity to offer any help. I was literary drowning in the doctrine of hatred, hating myself and the world.

As I continued walking, my legs led me to an abandoned bench where men always met to discuss politics and took some little *chan'gaa*, a local beer, for the day. The heaviness of my head gave way to sleep. I then supported my head on my bag and dozed off.

"Oh! Mummy, please don't let me come to this cruel world, please mummy do not allow me to face you to suck your succulent breast and suffer in the uncertain world; don't let me come in the world where politics rule the world, where I shall be judged by my tribe but not my character. Mummy please let me stay in your womb where I get all I need, where I am peaceful and I eat to my fill, smiling always and kicking to remind you of my presence. Where I roll and play as I want, sing my mornings and embrace my nights, never getting to hear the deafening gunshots and the rhythmic cries. Mummy please let me stay in your womb, mummy will you?"

Something scratched my legs; I then realized I was in a deep dream hearing my son speak. His voice was real.

I was awakened by a man and a woman talking in low tones. The drama before me faded away and I realised that the hours of the sun were gone, even as it emitted the last orange strips from the heavens fading in the west. The humiliation and the stigma I faced in school made me feel like I should not live again. The atmosphere of excitement that would be there in my childhood was not there anymore. I dragged my legs as I headed to my barrel of wilderness I called home. My heart skipping a beat for what lay ahead was uncertain.

The next morning was on a Saturday. I woke up after six o'clock in the morning. I had a headache and a stomach ache. I suspected it must have been cold food

I had eaten at dinner. Everybody was still on the pieces of rags spread on the wooden structures in the tent. These they had called bed for two years and counting. The two structures, one for my uncle and the other one for the children had always given us the comfort in their own standard.

I suspected I was sick or tired. I felt like vomiting but it was held back. Staggering in the room, I hit my leg on the stool and landed on a metal plate. The soup of green vegetables and tiny crystals of "meat" stained my dress. The floor, a rough course earth soft and very slippery, pulled me down again. I was thirsty and I was heading towards the water.

On the wooden shelf; one of the furniture my uncle managed to salvage during the run and placed at the corner of the tent where the kitchen was, there was an aluminum *sufuria*, cooking pan that had served us for some time now and cooked all the food we ate. Far left was a plastic bucket that kept the "clean" water. I drunk not one but three cups and my thirst subsided restoring my energy.

"Who is that?" Agneta my uncle's wife pulled the curtain. She looked at me from bottom to top and then from top to bottom. She looked like a bomb just about to explode.

"Take the clothes, go to the stream and wash them," she ordered.

The combination between Agnita and uncle Mwema was incomprehensible. Agnita was a cruel woman by all standards she was always bitter in life. Her character, her choice of words revealed her cruelty. If I were to choose whom to stay with, then certainly I would not choose Agnita. Uncle Muema was a polite man and a complete opposite of his cruel wife. "I said go wash the clothes you filthy good for nothing girl," She uttered furiously. The feeling of hatred was haunting me; I felt embarrassed and looked like a monkey that had seen the wrath of rain. I was going to wash clothes kept for a whole week!

"What about Kanini, can I go with her?" Kanini was uncle Muema's eldest daughter.

"Shame on you! Get off and go wash the clothes" I got out and found a pile of dirty clothes staring at me.

I leisurely picked them and put them in a basin. The tiny soap for the hundreds of clothes gave a staring look at the clothes as if complaining. Kanini, a high school student in one of the day schools in the camp, was still enjoying her sweet sleep. I hated my mornings and dreaded my nights. *What! Did it matter even if I complained?* I had no choice but to obey. Clad in a faded and tattered long blue jeans skirt and a purple T-shirt, I reluctantly headed to the stream.

Though it was difficult walking through Busu Tamu, I was used to it. I had to jump the broken sewers that emitted its contents. Watch children relieving themselves behind their doors, men empting their bladders too in every corner, cross the drainage system that passed near people's doors and tolerate the stench from the dumpsites.

Many activities went by; children were playing, men were drunk with words and local brew, and they danced and cursed. There was a group of people discussing politics and arguing. There were those that were fighting and gambling. All kinds of trade that one would mention went going on there. Women were selling the only thing they truly owned and the men who were willing buyers, ready to buy. Anything in skirt was an endangered species, too willing to risk for it came with a reward; earnings for a daily living. Boys too sailed in the same ship.

The world around was so beautiful and the creator had a lot of reason for his creations but I suppose the world had been made dangerous by the people and swaying away from the creator's purpose of creation. I could see children playing without boundary of tribe and culture. They were running up and down oblivious of what lay ahead. I wished I too had a chance to play *kati* and *Katolo* or *blada* and *bano* I wished I could remind myself, *dame* and *duduf mpararo*. I wished I made the planes and fly them up the sky. I wished I made dolls and nursed them and fed them but my childhood had been cut and soon I would be a mother to raise my child in wisdom and stature. My journey towards adulthood had been made shorter than I expected, so fast than I could imagine and the life within me reminded me of that.

After my duty of washing the clothes, I could not realize how fast time had moved soon the scorching sun was overhead and burning with all its fury as its golden rays pierced through the cloudless sky. My legs took me towards a log near the stream. I then imagined a peaceful world some day. A world where there would be no tribalism, war, racism and terror. Where people would embrace each other and the children of the world would enjoy the fruits of their parents' labor.

Mostly I wished that I never came into this cruel world and that I remained in my mother's womb. I would not have a name that contrasted my fate and hear gunshots every day that deafened my ears. I would not hear my mother complain about the crunching economy, I would not think about my father that I never got to see. I would not see the images of dilapidated bodies that were unidentifiable, Images that kept pressing hard in my mind. I would not hear the songs of hate and rage and dance to its tunes.

I would be peaceful, eat to my fill, smile always and kick to remind my mother of my presence. I would roll and play as I wished. I would sing my mornings and embrace my nights. Now I mourned my mornings and shunned my nights. Now I had to choose my friends and limit my play. But I still had a chance and all was not lost... as in the poem (I still have a chance). I then saw some two children running after each other; one picked a flower and hid it behind her back.

"Surprise!" she uttered giving the flower to her friend.

"Where did you learn that?" Her friend asked.

"I saw it on television. It expresses friendship", She replied. Her friend carefully took the flower and held it nicely in his hands.

"Thank you", He said.

Within a blink of an eye, she disappeared. He looked around to see where she had gone but to no avail. As if lonely in the park, he called her name. She was gone and the echo of her name came back. He looked ahead and saw her waving going with her mother. The fragrance of the red flower left her memory lingering in the head of the young boy.

Opening my eyes from the little day dream the time to head back to the camp had come. The golden rays of the sun were closing the business of the day, just about to let the moon and the stars take over for the entire night. I then put my load on my head and slowly carried my body back to the camp. My fingers were white and pale, my waist so tired and my tender womb overwhelmed by the growing size of my baby.

At my uncle's place, I had been reduced to a house help, waking up very early in the morning to do all household chores ranging from cleaning and preparing meals for the whole family. My uncle's wife was a busy woman who would attend *chamas* from one village to the other. The only time I got to see her was on Saturdays or Sundays. My uncle, Pastor Muema, had always been busy preaching the Good News of God. He was the man who gave hope to the internal refugees in the camp. This of course came with a daily living. He was a self pronounced preacher who had dedicated his life in preaching the word of God after losing his accounting job during the war. My uncle's family Bible was a heavy, canvas bound and with a zip. It had leaves that had known his hands for years. Every time he opened a verse from it and read it loud for us to hear. He then shouted trying to explain the verse he had read.

That evening as I ate food on the table, my stomach forcefully emitted the contents of the food. I supposed my body was beginning to experience the change that comes with pregnancy. I then rushed outside in the moonlight. "You don't seem to be alright, are you?" Agneta asked as if ready to help. Though I lived with my uncle and his family, it was not out of will or choice for the cruelty of her wife had always drifted me away from her. One would expect her to act like my real mother than she did. She looked at me as if she had never seen me before as my eyes gave way to the rain of tears. "Are you pregnant?" she hit the nail on the head. It pierced my heart and cut across my body. I looked at her and then nodded my head in probative. "What! I warned you about men, I knew you were pregnant! Abomination! Blasphemy! That cannot happen in the house of God," she uttered as she headed back in the tent she called house.

She was wailing like an ambulance carrying a patient to the Intensive Care Unit. She then came out again shouting. I cursed my condition and wished to tell her what transpired. She then slapped me heavily almost rendering me unconscious and dragged me in the house. "See, I told you, she is not a straight forward child. Now look! Her mother is no more and now she is about to bring a creature in this world to suffer just like her. Not in my house!" she said.
"What is the commotion all about?" Uncle Muema asked in a soft voice.

"What is the commotion all about?" She echoed uncle's voice.

"Can't you use your eyes and see that she is pregnant?" she said.

Though I had kept the secret one month and some days, the cat was out of the bag. "I don't want to see you near Kanini; she will be pregnant like you. If I ever see you near her, I will crush you like the bedbug you are." She warned. This phrase stuck in my mind like heart and soul as I headed to bed having not eaten anything for the night.

My night was long and I could not contain the noise in my head. I then got out in the wee hour of the night to watch the moonlight set as I thought of what was ahead. At age thirteen, I believed that the burden I was carrying was too heavy for me. I rested my head on the door pole and watched.

What was in my vicinity was nothing new for the life in the camp was growing worse day after day. People were still walking around and what was in my sight was worse than evil. It was an old sort of a concert that was not worthy a show. My brain remained unsettled and seemed to be suffering as if I had been given a morphine injection, the wish of finding my father become real and it was only a matter of time for me to embark on the ultimate journey.

The heavens then opened up unexpectedly and what was seemingly a simple rain grew to a heavy rain. It had not occurred to me that there would be such a downpour. Within minutes, it seemed terrible. My foot went down in water, another step and another and water kept rising. My wish was that it did not over flood for whenever it did, it was impossible to live in the internal refugee camps.

"Zawadi... Zawadi... Zawadi...!" the voice came through the rain, seemingly far away and barely audible. Then within seconds, Kanini's image presented itself in front of my eyes.

"What are you doing in the rain at this hour of the night?"I inquired.

"Lets get in, it is a long story," she uttered. She turned her face and waved; I saw a figure of a man waving back but could not know who that was. I then considered not to indulge my curiosity in the small scene as the two of us got in the muddy tent we called a house.

6

ONE MONTH LATER, things became worse. My
relationship with uncle Muema and his wife Agneta
dwindled by day. Going to school was now almost
impossible and the baby growing in my womb gave me
real nightmares. Facing Mr. Kisu everyday was so

horrific; his image made me feel like the world was coming to an end. It was like I was wondering in the wilderness for forty years. My intellect could not hold the nightmares, my stomach was now protruding showing that my baby was growing two months and counting.

My relationship with my peers at school had dwindled and changed thanks for the life in me which denied me the joy of my childhood. I was now in solitude. I was like a man sailing a boat alone and the boat is suddenly attacked by furious winds.

I must remove this creature before it takes over my life, my thoughts confirmed. At school, I watched my peers play and none was willing to let me join in their game. I was a poor girl left alone in the cold. It was as if my pregnancy was spelling doom for my entire life.

"Zawadi," Agneta's voice called behind the curtain. "Today I shall inform the school that you are pregnant," she said as she got out of the bed. My uncle was still asleep.

"They already know," I answered.

"And they are doing nothing about it; you cannot be in school in such a condition. You are showing a bad example to your peers," she said.

Within minutes, she held my hand and we dashed to school.

"Is this what you are teaching your pupils? *Enh*! Tell me, tell me *bwana* head master," she burst out in anger showing the headmaster my protruding tummy.

"Calm down and have a seat," the head teacher calmed her.

"Now tell me the whole story,"

I narrated the ordeal, it was like it was happening again. This time not practically but theoretically.

"No, Mr. Bokisa can't do such a thing" He cleared his throat and said.

"I know him as a respected teacher" He continued. I was literary gazing at him like a statue.

"You know girls of today can fix and pin labels on men, besides why didn't she report early?" He asked.

They decided to call Mr. Bokasa to tell his side of the story.

My heart skipped a beat and I knew facing that lion of a man in the name of Mr. Kisu was real death.

Should I run away from school? No! Not me. I gathered courage again. There was grave silence, and then my baby in the womb asked me to keep quiet for I could not hold the pain anymore. Nobody could fight for me. After a long discussion and Mr. Kisu declining to give his side of the story, blaming it all on the people he claimed wanted to finish him, I believed for a moment that there was no justice for me.

"Ok *Bwana mkubwa*, the big man, talk to her, tell her I don't want to see her near my daughter else..." Agneta said leaving angrily.

I then believed that there was eminent danger. I had to get out and look for my father for maybe he would fight for me and my assailant would be brought to book. Mrs. Wambete then led me to the guidance and counseling office. She looked at me and her black pupils behind her membranes showed a great pity she felt for me, she looked at me helplessly. She opened her draw and handed me a letter. "Don't worry my daughter all shall be well," She said. I looked at the letter as she closed her drawer, pulled out the staple and the largest handwritten font shouted from the paper:

Due to your condition you are hereby suspended from school until further notice.

After reading the letter, I folded it and headed to Mr. Kisu's office. I had vowed to let him pay for his sins though it was not seen.

"Yes young girl what can I do for you?" He asked. A moment of silence then followed. My heart was now bursting with anger and hatred as I stared at the forceful father of my son. I dug deep inside my bag and removed a knife. He drew near trying to take away the knife from me but I looked like a wounded lioness ready to show the world that I ruled.

"Let us talk about it," He uttered.

My mind could not give room for consultations or negotiations. When a social being is suppressed to the very end, the suppressor must expect a counter reaction. For a moment, my mind confirmed that I was the custodian of the teacher's life, and that someday my son would demand to know the father.

No! Not again. If I leave him, he would do to others what he did to me. I have to do something, I thought.

"I swear that I won't bother you anymore, but please put it down," He pleaded.

He reached out to my hand and took the knife. My hands were now wet, my tears rolling down and I discovered that my destiny was endless bitterness. Slowly I recollected myself and left his office, promising myself that someday I would get justice. I headed home.

"What do you want here?" Agneta asked.She pushed me away and my uncle came to my rescue.

"What is the commotion here all about? Leave the young girl alone." My uncle was now holding me and I felt a little secure.

"This is our daughter," Uncle Muema said.

"Our daughter indeed! I will count one to five and when I open my eyes this immoral girl should be out of my sight, two "women" cannot live in this house," she said as she advanced and threw my bag that contained all my earthly belongings at me.

"One… two… three… four…"

Before she counted five, I was already out of the house in the cold of the night. After a few minutes, my uncle persuaded me to get in the tent. He held me by the hand as we got back for the night. For the umpteenth time in my life, I woke up in the middle of the night only to find Kanini out again but only her shape in the structure we had called bed. On most occasion Kanini used to spend most evening away from home. She had played the trick on her father and mother for a long time.

Two weeks later life was not the same in my uncle's house. Agneta had always tried to persuade me to terminate my pregnancy as a condition of living with her. She believed that I was a disgrace in "God's family," To my horror, she warned me never to set foot in my Uncle's church. I wondered why she wanted me do away with the pregnancy, but I was getting convinced day by day. The reality of her words kept pressing, and for once, I agreed with her opinion.

She suggested a visit to 'doctor' in the camp without my uncle's knowledge. This was going to be a top secret that would never be revealed. As I deliberated upon it that night, I felt a pat on my back. I looked up and met face to face with Agneta.

"Zawadi...Zawadi... let us get out, I will help you remove the baby," She whispered. Her words cut across the darkness in the wee hours of the night. She put her hand in the pocket and removed a cell phone. She then dialed a number.

"Relax, he will be here in a short while," she said. Confusion was written all over my face. *Who is this he?* I asked myself. Within a short while, a tall and gigantic man came.

"Here he is, he will show you how to do it," she whispered.

I looked at him closely; he resembled a man Kanini had introduced to me as her boyfriend – whatever that meant. The man used to bring Kanini back home in the middle of the night.

I slowly picked myself up and met the man purported to be the doctor to help me do away with the creature in me. I looked at him and saw death than life. He was in his full regalia of white overcoat, some blades and white gloves. Around his neck, hung a metallic string that glistened like ghostly eyes in the dim moonlight. His loose fitting shirt gaped open to reveal his hairy chest, his right trousers leg rolled to the knee the other torn at the left knee and the right sleeve rolled up to the elbow ready for action as we walked slowly in the middle of the night going to his "clinic."

"I can't," I uttered

"Give yourself courage, courage Zawadi... Courage," Agneta said. Soon we arrived at the clinic; it was within the IDP camp.

My eyes then began to survey the carnivorous room; it did not resemble any shape. The ceiling was barely six feet supported by a tall pole that went through the roof and tied with a string. The other walls were supported by tired *fitos* small sticks. I wondered who on the outside would not believe that the room was where would be lives were cut short for it was a replica of mausoleum. *I am just few seconds away from freedom and this creature growing in me shall set me free, I* thought.

"We shall remove it and throw it in the bin nobody will ever find out," The Doctor said, his voice roaring like a rumbling cloud.

I looked at Agneta she looked directly into my eyes and whispered "it's time." I felt her hands caressing mine just to give me courage.

"Please keep it as a secret I am only trying to help you," she said. The doctor gave me a glass of a concoction full of some non familiar drink. I held it in my hands and looked at it.

'Take it,' he said. *Drink it*, I told myself. *You have nothing to fear.* Then a voice whispered in my heart: *"Zawadi do you seriously want to terminate the life of an innocent being?"* Just then my body began to shake to the roots of my being, and my mind began to replay all the consequences that I learnt about the termination of a pregnancy: *High chances of being infertile...HIV/AIDS ...living in guilt forever...*

"Take it," the Doctor said, placing his hands on my shoulder. The rays of the moonlight that weakly penetrated through the tiny holes of the ceiling presented a creature that I had known as my cousin in my eyes. Oh! Heavens I could not believe that Kanini was laying on the other side of the earthen floor writhing in pain. My heart began to pound wildly. The room had fallen deathly silent.

"What are you doing here?" Agneta asked her daughter in total disbelief. She stood appalled as their eyes met. Confusion raged the whole room. *My God!*

Then as quickly as it came a shrill of cold blood ran through my spine, my legs shivered and got an overwhelming energy. I dashed off like I wasn't three months pregnant. The episode left my mouth wide open and still could not believe what I heard and saw. It was now evident and crystal clear that I had to run for my life. *Off in this cask I call home, I must pursue this voyage of discovery in quest of my father and identity.* I thought. Perhaps it was time to begin the ultimate journey.

7

THE ULTIMATE JOURNEY and the long search for my father began a search for my identity. *When I find him I will tell him about Mr. Kisu, the teacher who made me drop out of school.* I thought. I would let him know that were he there, may be I would have a chance to get justice for my assailant was now walking scoot-free. I would teach him that love knows beyond tribe and the curse of tribalism should not have been the reason for him to leave my mother. Running away was like building a wall of mud to hold raging waters but the wall cracks letting threads of water through it without a sound.

I made the first step out in the middle of the night and the last watch of Busutamu camp ran over my eyes. Internally displaced, for we were refugees in our own country and the pangs of tribalism which had been attached to the people like a secret, had taken its toll and its effects, and passed from one generation to another. The journey to the unknown proved harder that night but the prospects of living in that barrel land I called home meant death.

As I walked down the terrain, the atmosphere was just too quiet. The birds of the air were all gone to sleep save for the barking dogs. The night was dark and there was no sign of the moon but the cold weather that was eating my flesh. There were some sounds though I could not figure out what they were. Then some footsteps, the footsteps became louder and louder. I thought I saw images of people but when I looked again there was nothing. Still fear had taken its toll and now I felt a silent threat like a cloud over the sun. Looking behind, I came face to face with terror and death.

Seven men, to be precise, carrying machetes and clubs stopped me. They lit a spotlight direct into my eyes. I stood freezing, not making a move and the baby in me froze too; I could not hear him leap. The men smelled death and one could see murder in their eyes. But it was the dried blood-stains spread across their tattered clothes that rendered me speechless. My heart began to pound and my mouth went dry as pepper. I looked at them again straight in their faces. The trouble I was going through was piling upon me as the waves rolls over the beach.

What have I got to lose? I told myself. It was better to face fear than to live in it. In the quietness of the night, one of the men grabbed me by hand, just about to shout he put something in my mouth. I did not know what it was, in a moment, I became unconscious.

When I regained consciousness, I found myself lying on top of a dumpsite. One would imagine what became of me and why I decided to sleep there. It was in the morning and I could not control my tears that had known its channel like a train on a railway line. The memory of my mum was pressing like she was alive.

I had always imagined that my memory of her was bound by the actual time we had spent together but this period growingly faded and her memory grew mysteriously stronger. The face of my mum was always in my eyes and any woman I saw passing by I would always imagine it was her. I kept her picture safe in my book; I talked to it, I kissed it and I would kill with my bare hands anyone who would dare take it away from me. I loved it!

In my memories, she could talk to me calmly in soothing voice that made me forget my troubles. She would touch my hair, and save me from many dangerous spots. She joked, smiled with me and laughed with me; she smiled at me and stared at me. I had only to close my eyes and hold my breath; feel the contact of her soft hands caressing mine.

In mixed reactions, the happiness of remembering my mum mixed with the pain of bringing Mr. Kisu to my memory. The man I had called teacher for long, *why then would he do that to me?* Then, I was heavy with his son, *how then would he find his identity?* I was supposed to sit for my final examinations, national examination which would define my destiny. I was too young to become a mother. The image of Mr. Kisu was pressing; the mathematics lesson in his office struck my heart. The ordeal that led to my condition chilled me when I thought of it the moment of the neighbors' killers, pressed again and again. I remembered watching people drop dead at Changaraweni, I remembered women being stripped naked and ravished in the full glare of their children. I remembered how a stuck of bodies, formed a wall with their hand tied behind, looking as if they were fighting for freedom and maddened me when I dreamt of it.

The pain of the tribal clashes that rendered me an IDP was pressing too I was labeled Internal Displaced Person in my country. I had always wanted to live in the good old days that everyone treasured, but I was not alive. The tentacles of tribalism, war and terror had gripped the people and the children learnt it as their first lesson in school. My prayer was that someday the madness shall be gone and I would land in the free light of peace and safety of a new bright age.

That day would begin when I get to meet my father. The ultimate price would be paid for I would let him stand by me by crook and hook.

The memory of my mum washed away the pain of remembering Mr. Kisu and the episodes of Changaraweni and Maporomoko . I could carelessly throw myself to my mum to hear the intonation of her voice cuddling my ears. The memory of her figure paralysed my thoughts, brought out the power in me and rendered me powerless. Her image had accompanied me for she was the treasure and secret which I could bring to life at will. I treasured the company of this invisible friend who winged her way to me so fast when I called her. I had more excuse for the little abatement for as I was certain never to see her again. What did it matter? My memory stabilised and I began to remember the night after the seven men who had now put me in the condition I was. They ran away with the little luggage I had carried from my uncle's place that contained all my earthly belongings, if any.

I believed they never harmed me. I did not know whether to cry or to face the bitter truth. My hands held a small black polythene bag. Digging deep inside, I realised that my mum's picture was not there. I was not sure whether to cut short my journey or to continue. A dark cloud was hanging around me and my journey seemed tougher.

Life seemed to be a sort of a monster or a symbol representing a monster of a form. It was like I never lived, but half dead, I was a rotting seedling. The worry of my livelihood overshadowed my reason for living. My internal noise was much more than the deafening sounds of *vuvuzela*. I gave myself courage and beat my chest. I was now standing in front of a building in town. My eyes were blinded by the streaming traffic and the sneaky traffic jam. *How did I get here?* I asked myself. As if I was grounded there with my hands on my cheeks and my head too heavy with thoughts, the hopes of finding my father were going with the wind.

The prospects of continuing with my studies were gone with the wind too. The thoughts of wasting my years of school overcrowded my mind. The thought of the pregnancy that at one time never came in my mind overwhelmed my life too. I was now shaking my head as if I was barmy; the madness in me had now taken full possession of me. I had always been a top performer in my school and all I wanted was the best. I had once read in a book that an idea is the driving force of desire. That as a man thinks so he is. I once read in a book that the world is kind, that what we needed was in the universe, and the law of attraction works best to those positioned to receive. *What says you my soul?* I asked myself.

My heart turned fondly to myself and I counted the blessings that I had received; I appreciated the gift of life given to me for free by my creator. I had thought of taking away my life and that of my little baby. I had known that whether thirteen or thirty-one, I had to live for something bigger than myself. My destiny was beyond my problems.

Still standing and putting my thoughts in order for I was a lonely girl in the crowd, the sun was right up, making faces behind the veil of a thin layer of clouds. A dark blue Mercedes Benz drove and stopped next to my legs. My eyes were permanently glued on the magnificent car. It took a while before I knew the occupants of the vehicle. Before I could blink my eye, a young lady opened the front door of the car and come directly to me.

She looked like she was in her early thirties. She was dressed in a maroon skirt and a matching blazer with a white blouse. Her face was pale and dark in complexion. She had a black handbag that matched her dress and her blonde hair was hanging loosely behind her bag. Her earrings glittered reflecting her beauty; she smiled at me exposing her deep dimples that the creator sunk in her face.

The golden necklace went round her smooth neck and dropped on her chest; she was a real model! In her hands were the car keys and her smooth legs dwindled down her skirt to the high heeled shoes as she came directly to me. Caught in the act of staring at her and literary drooling over her, I froze with fear for I had never seen such a beautiful woman in my entire life. I stared at her like a statue.

"Young lady how are you?" her smooth voice caressed my ears. Our eyes looked at each other for one second, and then mine dropped. It was as if she had not noticed my protruding tummy.

"Fine, thank you madam," I replied with millions of questions flowing in my mind.

"Do you know where Hakuna Matata Hotel is?" She asked.

Hakuna Matata Hotel was a renowned hotel in the city. I wondered why such a beauty queen did not know where the hotel was.

"Do you?" She asked again. I answered in the affirmative as if I was in my own world.

"Well, go straight along the Ngala Road turn le...," "Please take me there," She requested. "I...I...am afraid of strangers," I remarked. I was reluctant but after her assurance that she was not a bad person, my heart was convinced. I agreed and got into the car. I sat in the soft leather seat, I loved it. I was sitting all alone in the enormous back seat of the Mercedes Benz, Struggling out of the semiconscious day dream.

The Dark blue shelter eased away from the buildings and moved down the Banda Street. In the background the soft music at the back hummed evenly, as we headed to Ngala Road. The snaky traffic jam made us think otherwise.

"We are on the final stretch," I uttered as we went down to Accra road past the Times House to Mambo Leo building that housed Hakuna Matata Hotel.

The twenty storied building was an icon in the city for it was perfectly architectured. The car taxied its way to a parking somewhere in the vast expanse of the parking area. As my feet touched down I felt a rising excitement, *breath in, breathe out* I thought. It was more a dream than a reality. We were ushered in by a guard dressed in a large robe. We then stepped in the luxurious interior of the hotel. The deafening silence in the hotel revealed the kind of visitors she received.

"Hello please may I help you?"A soft voice echoed from our table; it was time to order our meal. I then ordered for chips and chicken and my guest ordered for beef served with *Ugali* – African stiff porridge made of corn.

"Welcome to the city, madam,hakuna matata, no trouble" I uttered. She smiled.

"Thank you, my name is Purity Maua of Soul Builders' Peace Corps," she broke her silence. I watched in silence trying to figure out what that meant to me, next to me was a renowned figure I had heard about for some time. I could not imagine that I was sharing a table with such a famous woman.

"I...I... am Zawadi Simba." I replied.

"So why are you not in school young girl?"She asked looking directly at my protruding stomach. My deep silence confirmed to her that I was not willing to share for she was pricking my wound and it started bleeding.

"It is fine, all shall be well", she said as she gave me a white handkerchief to wipe my tears. In a moment I gave her a section of my autobiography.

"...And that is my story," I concluded.

"So the teacher was never put behind bars?" she sought to confirm.

"Yes," I nodded my head in affirmative.

"Poor young girl so tender to be a mother, so where is your father?" She asked.

"I have no idea, all I know is that he is alive somewhere. His name is Ben. "...Ben?" that name ... she uttered suspiciously.

Purity Maua gave me a lot of encouragement that I needed at the time. It was like I was being led by an unseen hand which took mine while another hand reached ahead and prepared the way for me to meet her. Hers was a story of hope and the saying 'a cat has nine lives' applied greatly in her life. She narrated her story to me in the hotel:

"A Few years ago I had a strong organisation in my village. I had beaten all odds to become a woman leader. I had housed more than one thousand women and children, magnificent building and great support. The crude hands of the arsonist changed everything. They burnt and hacked them in the name of politics." she paused and continued. "After general elections, there was a crisis in the country. The Devil invaded the land, there was war everywhere and so people came to find refuge in my children's' home but that was their death place. Women were sexually assaulted, children sexually molested, my property looted and some reduced to ashes. Today my children's home is a grave yard." She wiped her tears. "Don't worry," I encouraged her too.

It then dawned on me that men and women are not exceptional when it comes to afflictions and sufferings. "I was not spared either. I was assaulted too. But my daughter life has to move on," she concluded smiling.

The mentioning of the word assault reminded me of what I went through in the hands of Mr. Kisu. "I am very delighted to meet you young girl, you are really a symbol of hope and I would be happy to take you to my new home, till your time comes for delivery. I hope you will come with me" "I will also try to help you find your father." She said. I could not believe my ears! Such an opportunity was handy. She was now going to be my confidante and dependent. She then paid the bill and off we left. My nerves had been set on the edge, my temples throbbed, and my life had been a nightmare. My heart was beating fast. But God had to send Purity Maua to be my Angel and comrade. My nerves settled and my temples stopped throbbing. I was sure of my child's safety and the remaining five months would be much of anxiety though in a quiet and a nice place.

My life had been a walk in a desert in a long dry spell but Purity Maua had provided an oasis that had changed my life and that of my baby boy. I felt like one who had had her violin out of tune with the orchestra and at last was in harmony with the universe, even as I proceeded with the mission of finding my father. We then left for Purity's home which was fifteen kilometers from the city.

8

PURITY'S HOME stood beautifully at the northern part of the city. The green gate was full of life and newness. As we made our way into the compound Mr. Mawindo, a guard as I came to know him ushered us in in the compound. He was dressed in his full combat; he was round faced and well built in his hands was a club perhaps to scare away the enemies. Purity packed the car at the garage and off we headed to her house. I stood frozen in the door way of the beautiful house and studied the splendid scene before me. I glanced through the floor –to-ceiling.

The floor had a woolen carpet whose origin I did not know. Up on the eastern wall of the living room was dominated by pictures and artistic designs hanging on the cream wall. The calendar stood still on the western wall which was equally decorated and a statue of a Maasai moran was leaning against it. The entire room had precisely arranged furniture. The ceiling was a vast expanse of soft board with a series of dramatic light fixtures that threw a muted glow upon the cream colour of interior finishes. Up the stairs were pictures too.

My new found home at Purity's house, gave me the peace that I had desired by day. Life was seemingly providing the needed happiness and now I felt like I had a great mother I felt like I was beginning it all over again, however I was saddened by the fact that I still had along way to get my father. I now began to understand that love is the most important thing in life.

"So how will you get your father?" she asked as we took breakfast in the beautiful living room.

"I am yet to know," I replied.

"Poor little girl" She said. Her eyes glistened with tears and now her voice started to falter. Looking straight into her eyes it was like she was asking a question worth a million answers.... "Why has this happened to me?" It was not answerable. Now my eyes were glued to her with some sort of compulsive fascination.

The similarity between us in the drama that was unfolding began to count, not in looks, not in emotions but in almost all aspects of life. The difference between us was only that she was an adult and I was a child and that she was childless and I was soon becoming a mother.

Purity Maua was a great homemaker. The time that I had stayed with her, she had provided me with almost everything I had ever needed as a child in my age and as a prospective mother. She was good in cooking and cleaning and became my counselor and personal doctor whom I confided in and who treated my soul at will. I was like a daughter in that new found home.

Often Purity as I kept calling her looked at me with a lot of admiration and sometimes literary weeping. As we sat in the couch she kept looking at me time and again. "Why me?" she asked. I did not understand why she was doing that. Was it because she was childless? *But my presence should give her the joy of having a child*. I thought. She then squeezed my hand as she turned off the television and asked, "Are you sure you want to see your father?"

"Yes," I nodded.

The truth was that I was sure that it would be good for me not to look for him but I did not know if anyone going through what I was experiencing would say no.

"It would be better if I saw him and knew what he does. I know he is alive," I told her.

"Ok my love," she said caressing my ears as I rested my head on her palm.

"Should I get to see him, I will be complete and I will tell him all I have gone through," I continued.

She turned on the television which stood perfectly on the TV stand that was romantically embraced by a statue of a lion to the left and an Elephant to the right. Our eyes were glued at the continuing series of a soap opera called; *the promise*. Soon it was time for news. The headline was about a thirteen year old girl who died in the hands of her mother after she was thoroughly beaten for allegedly refusing to get married to an old man in exchange for three goats. The pictures flashed and a man old enough to be her grandfather came on the screen. The mother was covering her face with a scarf in shame fearing the pictures from the members of the forth estate. As the news anchor continued with the news, my eyes were glued on the television as I wrestled with the pain. Purity then left the room.

"I am going to prepare lunch," she said. Then my attention was brought back to the TV. A notch twisted in my stomach and painful memories flooded back. It was not so long ago that I went through a similar experience, for I was assaulted by the man I called teacher. I remembered how children tragically lost their lines in the hands of the people called to protect them. I remembered how children so innocent to know what was happening were subject to hard labor, terror and war – never given a chance to enjoy their childhood. I remembered the children at Busutamu camp whose dreams of a better tomorrow were shattered like glasses and pieces scattered with no glimpse of chance to put them together. The memory of Kanini came to me, as I saw her lie down griping with lots of pain trying to procure an abortion. I looked again at the TV. It was amazing how the news was trending in the social media as I began receiving messages from my facebook and twitter accounts. The world is indeed a global village.

"Is it bringing back memories?" Purity asked.

"A bit," I answered.

"Thank God that you are now doing well, you have to be strong and keep being positive!" She said as she put her arm around my shoulder.

"Not everyone is like you Zawadi; people face struggles in different ways. When you overcome you will realise how amazing you are. For now there is no other way to be," she continued.

I stared into space as I recalled the life at my uncle's place; the picture of children at Busutamu camp played in my mind – I remembered children even tiny toddlers had to beg and scavenge. Their destiny had been cut short by tribal wars and terror which innocently ate up their bodies and soul. Sometimes I would watch children bite into pieces of unidentifiable food. The innocent souls would go into the dirty streets to eat rubbish and sell scavenged items at the expense of their education.

Behind the wretched appearance and the hard life they lived, lay a great smile and destiny that only the likes of Purity Maua could reveal. I then remembered Agneta, the woman who almost cut short my baby's life. I remembered the life at school a few months ago. How every one evaded my company and denied me to play. Staring at my protruding stomach that was about to burst its contents, the pain of Mr. Kisu, the man whose blood was forcefully flowing in me came to my mind.

"Shall we turn off the TV?" Purity asked.

I realised that time had really flown.

"No, let us watch until the end." I said. We prepared to take dinner as we continued watching.

Time slipped by, and it was now two months since I went to that third home that was now seemingly better than the other two. Day by day I asked myself one major question that not even my fragile heart could hold.

Could Purity know my father? Or what secret does she have about me? I refused to make my mind think again and I let the thoughts go by the air. I remembered the photo and what was written behind it in bold, **"Purity when she was three months pregnant ..."** I shook my head and the thoughts evaded.

Living in the posh neighborhood of Lavin had changed my life. Everything was orderly and clean; the quietness   provided the inner peace and the green trees provided great scenery. Life in there was much better than at the camp. But the dilemma of finding my father eroded my happiness. The greenness and the quietness of that place could not fill the vacuum in my heart. I turned fondly to my baby, "Oh! How sweet will it be to see your first smile little baby boy."

I was seated by the pool looking at the little girls and boys playing in the pool. I had a wish that made the glands of my tears explode. If only I never got pregnant, I would live with the guilt of assault but never see its product.

"If I deliver you safely young man please be good, for I will always be good to you. I will let you play by my pool and let you fly your wings like the morning bird as you sing the morning dew away. I will fight for your rights and make you great." My tummy leapt and the little creature in me kicked. Soon a butterfly settled on my palm. This time my thoughts were not cruel. I let it "wing" it's winglets and gave it yet another chance to live. As if it had enjoyed my company, it went and called all like-minded butterflies. In a moment, the miniature birds became my friends and comrades spreading out the beauty in the world. My lips opened up and I produced an elegant smile as bright as the morning star and they too smiled back, we smiled and laughed at each other.

It was as if faith was beginning to give me the chance that life took away from me. I was longing to be free; this freedom would only come when I would see my father and tell him my story. One shoe can change your life, they say. My wish was that the whole earth would be united and people living on it would preach peace. My wish was that Mr. Kisu would be brought to book and all like-minded people, never given a chance to maim the promising lives of the children of the world. My freedom would come only if the curse went away and pronounced a great blessing and when the diversity of our tribes and culture would be a tool for unity and beauty. When we would all understand that differences in tribe, religion, color or race is not equal to enmity and division, but diversity and strength.

One Monday evening, I heard the sounds of the grand piano playing loudly. I knew Purity was upstairs for she loved playing it. The famous song filled the air and the writer of the song could not have done lesser work on it:

Amazing grace how sweet thy sound,
That saved a wretch like me,
I once was lost but now am found,
Was blind but now I see...

"You really play it so well Mum," I commented. She looked at me with an amazing smile for a friendly smile is always in style.

"Thanks baby. Do you want to try?" she asked. I then sat next to her as I watched her fingers press the keys so tenderly and softly.

"Not now," I uttered. Then some uncomforting silence followed. She broke the silence and asked.

"So what did you say is the name of your father?"

"Ben Simba," I answered.

"Did you ever get to see him?"

"No, he left my mother when she was pregnant with me, but my mother like I told you died in the tribal clashes"

"Tribe again why would one be judged by his or her tribe?" she asked me as if I knew the answer.

"So why aren't you married?" I asked. Rev.Purity rolled her eyes wishing I could ban that word.

"You are too young to understand," she said.

"Too young? But I am soon becoming a mother!" I replied.

"A mother in deed!" She uttered and smiled as if my being a mother was a joke. Sure it was, especially in this age and time. Though Purity was not married, she had a fiancé who came occasionally. His name was Abdi. Abdi was a kind man who always few of words.

He worked as a police pilot and was often in and out of the country.

"Yes am not married but soon I will be marrying Abdi. You see my daughter love knows not religion, color or race. In the eyes of God we are all equal.

She pulled me up by my hand and led me to the couch. She then opened a black thing that looked like a book.

"What do we call this?" I inquired innocently.

"It's called a tablet, a small computer that one can carry along" she explained.

"This is a gift for you; it will assist you to get any information you may need." I was not so sure why I felt like there was something Mum Purity, as I had been calling her, was hiding. I had already told her about my father and every detail that she would need to assist me in getting him, *why then would she still be asking me the same information?* Something stroked my chord and it was difficult to ignore it.

"Come and play baby", she called me back to the piano and left me playing my favorite song.

Everyday she offered to teach me how to use a computer and seemingly, I was becoming an expert and at per with my fellow peers of the current age and time. The tablet had become my companion and any time I felt bored, I could listen to music, type or chat on *Face book* and follow friends on *Twitter* and *whatsapp*. My pain was slowly coming to an end and seemingly I found myself in a little heaven. However, this did not go on for long. Purity's heart was more overburdened than mine and I failed to understand what was going on in her mind.

The thought of her not having a child made her heart faint and weak. The question I asked her had made her think and wonder why she had to go through the journey of life with such pain and rage. I suspected there was more than met the eyes.

In two months' time I would be out of danger. I would be bringing forth yet another creature in this world and my wish for him would be greatly fulfilled. I would be ready to guide him through the entire life. I thought.

That night was going to be the beginning of the ultimate change of my life for I had found a friend on Face Book. His name was Ben George. I liked him because he was seemingly wise and genius and he shared a name with my father. I could not miss chatting with him on face book every now and then.

"So what do you do for a living?" I posed a question and clicked the send button.

"I am a Priest in the Catholic church where I serve the Lord," he replied. Our conversation went on and on and one would think it was between father and daughter.

The burden in Purity's heart had made her to be in solitude for she was seemingly carrying one of the greatest secrets of her life. The tears that rolled down her cheeks by day and night left me worried. As we were seated on the table, she put her arm around my shoulders.

"My daughter, I have found another home for you which would provide the best grounds for your delivery; the Daughters of the Pure Heart Mission Home." She said. At first my heart declined but remembering how she had helped me I believed it was worth following her directives. My transfer to the Daughters of the Pure Heart home was one of the best choices I had ever made. When a tree falls near a river, use it to take you to the other side of the river.

A day before my departure to the Daughters of Pure Heart Mission Home, something unusual happened. Purity was very happy and accommodative. I was beginning to wonder whether she was happy that I was going to the mission center. As I went to the bedroom, she dropped a picture of a man and a woman at a university entrance. As fate would have it, I picked it and gave it a closer look. The man looked familiar but surprisingly the woman in the picture was Purity. As I held the picture, she grabbed it and sent me to the living room. I began to suspect something; the picture looked like the picture that was in my social studies book, the one that was stollen. I did not want to believe it was true, but something told me there was more in Mum Purity's blue eyes behind the picture.

"So you are alumnus of Kisuma University? That is the same University my mum was. I enquired.

"Yes! I am an alumnus of Kisuma University. I studied Political Science."

"What a coincidence! I think we share so much in common, don't we?"

"So many things indeed," she uttered rubbing her fingers on my hair.

I looked down deep into her eyes and saw the secret behind the eyes. *There must be something* I told myself. "My daughter, lack of love is the greatest sin. Always love your neighbor as you love yourself," She uttered as she drove me to the Daughters of the Pure Heart Mission home that would be my home till my delivery. After which I would be enrolled back to school to continue with my studies. I was happy to find someone to take care of me and Purity had proven to be a real mother. Though she had no children, she refused to get married for the only man she loved left her at the time of need due to tribal differences but there she was trying to collect rubbles and putting the pieces of her heart together, she was ready to give it another chance by marrying Abdi.

"You will come to know about it when you become of age," she said as we approached the Daughters of Pure Heart Mission home which was going to be my home for some time. There were girls who were in the same condition as I was. One would think it was a small women hospital. It was interesting to hear experiences from people who had gone through what I had considered the most traumatizing experience of my life. The mission was a haven of peace and beauty. The beautiful flowers and the nice old buildings brought back peace and satisfaction. She housed one of the biggest Catholic Church in the region; the Comboni Mission Church. The face of the church was appealing to every believer, giving them encouragement for an opportunity to proclaim faith.

Day in day out I could see men and women of all clothes, kind and unkind lingering about to give their confessions to the Priest. Father Maurice was one much respected person, very soft spoken and kind. He was well built in stature. In his late thirties, he was serving the church as a Priest for the second year, but he had been brought up in the church once as an altar boy and a youth leader. His humor during the service and outside made his followers always stream at the Comboni Mission church. My legs and feet had now mastered every corner of the mission school and convent.

I was now used to the blue gate, the front door through the wicket, the humps of green, the flash of flowers and the nuns who moved around either singing or carrying books to teach catechism. The grey scarf and uniform had now stacked in my mind.

"Why would "mum" bring me to a Catholic mission center?" My fervent prayer was that I meet the man behind my existence before I deliver.

Purity visited me occasionally to see how I was doing for now my bond with her had grown stronger than granite. The privilege of staying at the mission center had made me learn many things and my integration to the canonic way of life was seemingly great. Some times, I attended the mass and even practiced a number of activities in the mission center.

After one month, I was now a well-known figure in the Catholic Church. One month from then I was going to be a mother of a baby boy. Feeling my baby kick in my pregnant tummy made me smile, but the actual birth and the fact that I had not planned for my fate, made me worried. I was too young to go through that.

Many people called me *Zawa*, short for Zawadi. The children at the mission home now became my best pals. I loved living there. The peaceful environment and the psychological chastity of the sisters gave me encouragement. That whatsoever happens in ones life, the choices we make affect us a great deal. The ideas we have and the choices we make contribute a lot to the lives we live.

Sister Mary, one of the youngest nuns had developed a liking for me. She teased me around and even encouraged me at one time to join the congregation. I could say for sure I loved Sister Mary. Her calmness and politeness made me think of heaven. She was beautiful and decided to remain chaste.

One would wonder if in her own oblivion she would ever think of having a boyfriend, leave alone getting married. In the society young girls had been corrupted in their brains. Every time I met Sister Mary, she would tell me about herself and how good I was. Being her friend, she was someone I could trust at her age of twenty-two. She really felt that we shared a lot in common.

Sister Mary was sweet, very healthy, popular and good. She was happy all the times and contented at the convent. She was effortlessly clever and liked children. She was a slender, sweet tempered- baby, very pretty young woman. She had never been spoilt at least going by her words.

"Zawadi I am married to the church. I have decided to give God my life. My younger sister is almost getting married; my elder brother married and has one three - year pretty girl, young girls of today...," She said showing her warm radiant smile that revealed her milky teeth.

She never knew that sometimes I felt like not talking about the girls of today for at my age and time I was carrying a creature due to test the congested oxygen of the world.

"...they know so much that I don't know. I am chaste," She continued shaking her head to give way to the head scarf on her head that made her look like a small mother. From Sister Mary's account, it was a tale of tales, but behind the warm radiant smile laid a dark past that was eating her from the inside.

"I came from a rich family," she bragged.

Her father was wealthy. He worked as a Mechanical Engineer in town and her mother was a high school principal. She had all she wanted. She was uncritical of her parents and adored their posh home. She had been taken to a boarding school at the age of ten and was going out of childhood without spots and tantrums.

Life was seemingly flowing well like a river that had just left its source. People called her princess; she was an admiration of the whole estate including teachers and boys. Nevertheless, her innocence made no boy think of approaching her. She was unapproachable, book-worm and happy young lady. She acted like the sun spreading light all around when she came into a room.

"One Saturday evening I will never forget it," she said. It was a Saturday that changed her life, which took away the trust she had and replaced it with guilt and regrets. "That Saturday an extraordinary thing happened. I was tired. Having closed school I was at home alone; a sweet girl at sixteen.

My family had gone to a friend's party. After watching my favorite comedy *IN THE HOUSE OF BIG MAMA,* I went straight to my bedroom seemingly very tired. Thirty minutes into deep sleep, the bedroom door opened. I screamed to awaken the dead. In front of me was a man I had called daddy for sixteen years: a good well-educated man who had all it takes to be a responsible and understanding father and a very good caretaker. I couldn't just imagine", she uttered wiping her tears.

"He came directly to me with red eyes. I watched him make his advancement. In amazement my thoughts held ransom, imprisoned for life never to imagine what would befall me; he was a real attacker.

"Daddy please!" I exclaimed.

"Sh....sh....sh!" he whispered. He was a lion ready to pounce on a prey of the same blood.

"Daddy please ...!" I exclaimed and shouted. The man was oozing with sweat salivating ready to take the opportunity. He finally reached me. He grabbed my hands. I hit him hard and ran away. I was rescued by Purity Maua and I was brought here where I vowed never to get married."

Mary's story made my small baby kick. At least for her she managed to escape from the hands of her assailant. The kicking of my son coupled with Mary's story made me hasten the quest to find my father.

9

IT WAS PITCH DARK OUTSIDE, the alarm clock rung and the first cock crew to welcome yet another day. The birds of the air were singing their sweet melodious song as they chased the morning dew away and prepared to suck nectar. That beautiful

Sunday morning my son in my tiny womb kicked to remind me of his existence. "Good morning son! Welcome to the planet earth," He nodded his head in acceptance to my positive gesture to the planet earth.

For eight months, I had housed him in my womb and sometimes even thought of getting rid of him. For eight months, he had tried his level best to survive and stick by the laws of the womb. "My son as you come to the planet earth, you will spend most of your time chasing your dreams and collecting data. The data of what you want, you will realize that life is a phenomenal and magnificent trip that you alone will be the sojourner." The bright sunlight emitted its golden rays and the window curtain submitted to the strength of the rays allowing them to spread across the room.

It was mandatory to attend the mass at the Mission and so I had to prepare myself for prayers of the day. My supple knees landed on the floor as usual as I talked to my creator. Anxiety loomed for my time to meet face to face with death to give life; I wished that the cup of death was taken away from me.

Why should I hold the pain and drop the baby   when I can hold the baby and drop the pain? I encouraged myself as I put the finer details of my Sunday best.

The doorbell rung and I rushed to open. The warm radiant smile Purity displayed met with mine as we prepared to celebrate yet another beautiful Sunday.

"Welcome in mother" I said to her as if she was my real mother.   Surely, she was, for she had been a great mother to me.

"Sit down my daughter," she told me. My eyes were glued on her as if she was ready to throw a time bomb.

"One cannot keep a secret for long," she started as I waited the proceedings of the words.

"My heart has been overburdened for so long and the time to reveal to you the truth has come. When I first set my eyes on you in town, I shed tears and asked God why he allowed you to suffer that way. But I had to thank him though that he led you to my hands for I believed that what I had been missing in my life for all the years had come." She touched my palm and looked directly into my eyes.

"I am your real mother and your father's name is Ben," She said showing me the birth certificate and then

114

continued, "We lost contact at the university. He was studying Education while I was studying Political Science. I could not marry him because he was from a different tribe. Both our parents could not approve our relationship. We had shared a lot together; exchanged letters, went for outings and enjoyed each other's company. In the brilliance of our affection and youth, everything was blushing and good. Life was like a pot waiting to be poured in wine. The energy, the faith, the belief in the goodness of humanity and the love for mankind, made us feel like we were riding on a caring storm in which we alone were the passengers and the windstorm pushed our vessels to a greater destiny. We alone were the sojourners and the ones to define our lives.

We believed that we would live in love forever and the belief that one was born and one would die never made it to our minds. Our nickname 'the wonder birds' was the talk of the University. Every dawn brought us closer to the reality of our love. Our courtship was full of bubbles of joy that never faded. Every time we used to ask ourselves when exactly we would walk down the aisle, when our destiny would land directly into our hands and see the siblings smiling. Life was seemingly beautiful until hell broke loose," she paused. "I was pregnant with you. Three months into pregnancy, his parents would hear none of it. They threw me out in the cold of the night. I left crying and that was the last time we saw each other. I vowed to live my life. I contemplated securing an abortion but I respected life for I believed that someday you would be one of the greatest people in life, I gave you the chance to live and see the better of days." the story continued.

"My daughter, on my due date, I became unconscious and went in a coma. My friend Lawaridi was the one to take care of you. I entrusted you to her care and she took the responsibility willingly unfortunately she died in the hands of the arsonists. I was happy to see you again." She finished and hugged me tightly. I felt her tears flood my shoulder as well as mine. She then looked directly into my eyes and wrapped her arms around me.

So all along I have been living in falsehood thinking that Lawaridi was my real mother, I thought. Surely, it is your truth that shows who you truly are far more than your abilities. My weak body fell on my mothers shoulder as tears of joy rolled from my eyes.

Dreams never come true if you do not believe in yourself. The joy of knowing my mother made me a step closer to my identity, and the belief that my father was alive made my hope even stronger.

"You will be enrolled back to school once your child is born. For now I have great peace in my heart," she said wearing her famous smile. We were both so excited, but my worry about the actual birth made me even more scared. "You will be fine," she assured me.

She held my hand and took me to my room at the home. She then showed me many items she had purchased for my baby. "It would be better if I inform your uncle about us; I believe he has been troubled for long. He also thought that I was dead but I know he will be happy to see me again," she said. "Now my daughter, there is one more thing you should do. You have to forgive your assailants before your due date." The word "forgive" struck me like an iron bar thrown thirty feet from the heavens. The hatred and anger I had for Mr. Kisu could not allow me to think of the word forgiveness in my heart.

"My daughter forgiveness may not erase the past but will open a greater door for a better future. You will also find peace in your heart and justice for I have filed a case against him. When you forgive him you will reconcile with your child and when you leave the matter to the law of the state he will have paid for his sins. Forgiveness would open a greater door of opportunity in your fragile heart," she commented. "No! I can't; I can't face that goliath of a man even if his blood flows in my womb now about to erupt. He made me drop out of school. He is more than a murderer and setting my eyes on him to tell him that I have forgiven him will be more than committing suicide," I uttered in fury.

"My daughter I know you were deeply hurt, but it's eminent that you embark on the forgiveness journey, though rough but the best," she said. I looked at my mum's eyes and saw the need to forgive, as long as I found justice. She did it and the joy in her revealed just that.

"But how? Just how?" I asked her. "People come into your life to figure out who you are and teach you a lesson. Nothing happens by means of good luck, everything happens for a reason. And when you forgive you realise you have yet another world." She answered me. After a long deliberation I chose to forgive praying that justice will one day prevail in my life even as we prepared to embark on yet another journey.

10

THAT NIGHT MARKED the beginning of the end of my ultimate journey. I felt as if the baby was about to come out as I rested on my bed. My body was shaking and I was not sure of making it back to Busu Tamu and to Maporomoko Primary school. Within minutes I lapsed into a deep sleep. Then I was in the dream land.

It was on a Thursday morning; 10a.m to be precise and the court room bulged out her contents. This was the day I anticipated to finally find justice. I would be more than happy to see the man behind my troubles put behind bars. He was standing in the dock and in a black suit and a long tie that rested on his tummy. All my teachers and fellow pupils were present. Some of the parents had also managed to come.

"All rise!" the prosecutor brought the court to order. My heavy stomach pulled me down as I tried to stand but my mother supported me. "Just try," she said. The prosecutor then started the court proceedings. "Gentlemen of the jury, the suspect before this court is charged with child molestation. He is accused that on 12th January, he assaulted Zawadi Simba. Zawadi Simba, the plaintiff, is a minor, a thirteen year old girl whose future life has been cut in the bud. I therefore need to ask you to give this case the most serious and deliberate consideration; for the crime which he is charged is of the highest penal nature. It is a case of utmost importance to the public and to the accused. I shall best discharge my duty in this case by simply calling your attention to the facts which I shall prove in evidence." He said.

"First, on Friday January 12th, Zawadi Simba, who was a pupil at Maporomoko Primary school was excited to be in Mr. Bokasa's class. He was teaching mathematics. My lordship the victim had not understood the questions given and the accused asked for private remedial lessons with the victim. The victim was more than willing to participate in the remedial lesson due that evening.

The evidence points out that the teacher changed and became an assailant. In this case I have two witnesses to testify even as I look forward for justice to prevail. I wish to call in my first witness." The guard at the door called in a schoolboy. The school boy went to the bench and took the oath. The prosecutor proceeded to cross-examine the witness.

"In your own words, would you please tell this court where you were in the evening in question?" He asked.

"I was in class, everybody had gone home but I was left behind with some of my classmates to do our homework for we preferred finishing our homework at school. Zawadi had gone to Mr. Kisu as we called him...sorry Mr. Bokasa's office for remedial lesson on what she had not understood in class and promised to be back. When she took long to come back, and the rain had started falling, we became suspicious. We ran towards the teacher's office only to find her lying in a pool of blood on the floor and the teacher was shaking terribly. I believed that something bad must have happened." He commented as he concluded.

"Thank you! That will be all for now, I now call in the second witness," the prosecutor said. The second witness came to the bench and took the oath as well as it is the tradition in courts. The prosecutor then proceeded. "Could you please tell this court what you were doing in school at the hour of the evening yet it was not school time?" He asked.

"I love studying and we were preparing for national examination due at the end of the year, and you know our system requires that you pass national exams to go to the next level, so it was good to take some few minutes to study..." The prosecutor cut the second witness short then the witness proceeded...

"As I was saying my friend Zawadi went to ask a question in Mr. Bokasa's office which never was... she was lying in a pool of blood..."

The witness was now shaking and shading tears. "...I could see him... Yes! Mr. Bokasa shaking... he went and held her hand.... she could not breathe. Noticing that we had seen him, he left the office and threatened to harm us if we dared to report. We took the victim home in the young darkness. That is as far as I can remember" the witness said.

"Thank you," the prosecutor said.

"You may have your seat," he ordered.

"May the prosecutor cross examine the accused," the magistrate ordered.

"You are Mr. Bokasa?"

"Yes your honour,"

"Is it true that you assaulted that girl over there?"

"Your honour, I am a man of sound mind and I don't think I would do such a thing. May be I was tempted or was under influence of something," he said.

"So you were tempted?"

"I said maybe."

The whole court was full of scoffs. The prosecutor then proceeded, "Your Lordship, the crime here is big and to make matters worse it involves a minor. It is not a laughing matter, please let us get serious." The magistrate then spoke,

"Bearing the magnitude of this case I think we must now take a lunch recess. Court will reconvene at 2 o'clock this afternoon." He concluded.

Something scratched my tiny legs only to realize that I was in the middle of a long dream. I then sat on my bed meditating and praying for justice even as I anticipated for the journey back in the morning, hoping that my assailant would be brought to book someday.

The constant ticking drew my glance towards the clock. It was precisely 10 a.m. and my journey back to Maporomoko Primary School began. My heart was overwhelmed even as I got my comfort in our Mercedes Benz. The blue shelter within minutes took the ultimate journey in history; the journey to forgiveness. I was also going to let my assailant know that soonest he would be behind bars. We drove past Mamboleo Resort. Within minutes, we found ourselves at the Busutamu camp. Nothing had changed since I left four months ago, the people in the camp still lived against hope. I believed they too would find the art of forgiveness which is the greatest practice one can do. People's hearts were soaked in blood and hoping that one day, they would find justice. But that justice begins with forgiveness for when you forgive, you get the best justice in the world.

Our car drew much attention. Curious onlookers followed to see the occupants of the car. Women were dancing as men chased the car from behind hoping that we would "cough" something for the tummy. My mother lowered the front window and stopped the car right in front of Uncle Muema's tent. Agneta looked at my protruding stomach and shouted.

"Purity we thought you were dead. Oh!" She exclaimed.

"Where is Kanini?" I asked.

"She died while trying to procure an abortion?" she replied sobbing.

"What?" my baby kicked.

"My daughter, please forgive me," she uttered trying to kneel down but my mother stopped her. I looked inside her eyes and uttered "I have forgiven you untie." We then hugged one another so passionately like mother and daughter. One could not imagine the joy she felt after the forgiveness.

Moments later, we decided to walk to Maporomoko Primary School. The rough terrain could not allow our car to get there. My body began to shake as blood froze.

"Mum I can't," I said.

"Just try my daughter, we shall be there in a short while," She said. The green gate of Maporomoko primary school which was now in the vicinity reminded me of my condition. We then got to the school. As we were heading to the head teacher's office, I gained the courage of forgiving Mr. Bokasa. Mr. Bokasa entered into the head teacher's office. He was amazed to see me back and it was easy to see confusion all over his face. My mother's neck turned to him and what came to my ears was enough to deafen it. It was like watching another episode of a great movie.

"Purity!..."

"Ben!..."

The two voices met in the air, it was now clear that all that was eating my soul was part of me. "Ben Bongo Bokasa, so you are here, I mean you are the one....you are the assailant!" It then dawned on me that Mr. Bokasa was my real father. My baby kicked, my body became weak I dropped down like a sack; I guess I fainted. Within minutes I was wheeled into theatre and the caesarean process began. Moments later the surgeon reached inside my womb, gave a brief tug and lifted out a baby with the usual refrain:

"It is a girl!"

She was laid on my chest and I gazed at her in amazement.